Autumn
the Falling Leaves
Fairy

Special thanks to Kristin Earhart

To Madeleine and Abby, forever friends
of the fairies

ISBN 978-0-545-48495-4

12 11 10 9 8 7 6 5 4 3 2 1   13 14 15 16 17 18/0

Printed in the U.S.A.   40

First printing, September 2013

Autumn
the Falling Leaves
Fairy

by Daisy Meadows

SCHOLASTIC INC.

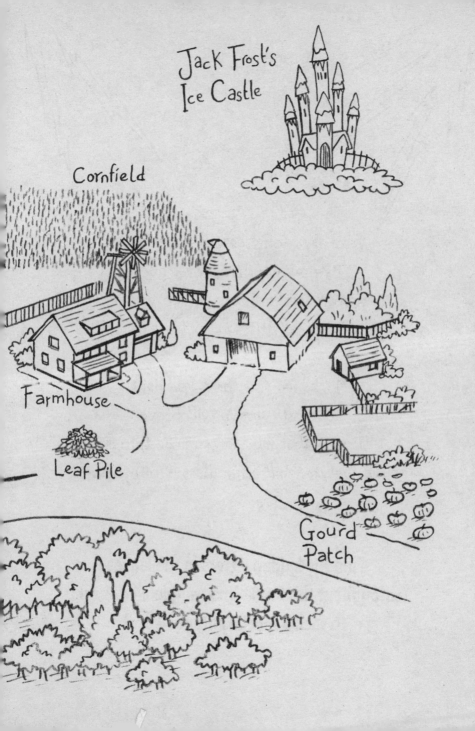

Why have four seasons every year?
I like my weather more severe.
Who needs autumn's golden leaves?
Who likes fall's first crisp, light breeze?

I like ice and snow and hail!
My frosty season will prevail.
I'll steal that fall fairy's magic things.
Now feel the chill an endless winter brings!

**Find the hidden letters in the leaves
throughout this book. Unscramble all 7 letters
to spell a special autumn word!**

A Brisk
Breeze

Contents

Down on the Farm

"We could not have planned it better," Kirsty Tate told her best friend, Rachel Walker, in the backseat of the Tates' car. "It's the perfect weekend for you to visit. The Fall Festival at New Growth Farm is going to be so much fun!"

Rachel nodded and gave Kirsty a bright smile. She could hardly get a word

in! Ever since she had arrived at Kirsty's house for the long weekend, her friend had been talking about the farm fund-raiser.

"There will be apple picking, arts and crafts, and a giant leaf jump on the  last day," Kirsty explained, too excited to sit still. She fiddled with her seat belt and swung her feet. "Kirsty, dear," Mrs. Tate said from the front seat of the station wagon, "I'm looking forward to it, too, but please stop kicking my seat."

Rachel giggled. It was funny seeing Kirsty so wound up.

Kirsty decided to use her energy to tell

Rachel more about the farm. "The best part is that my class has been going there on field trips," she said. "We feed the chickens, and help water and mulch the plants. We've learned a lot from Kyra, the farmer."

Rachel nodded again.

"I can't wait for you to see the orchards, and the rows of vegetables, and the duck pond. I know you'll love it all," Kirsty told her friend.

"It sounds like a magical place," Rachel said. She gave Kirsty a sly grin. After all, the two girls knew a lot about magic! They couldn't tell anyone, but Kirsty and Rachel were special helpers to

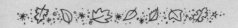

Queen Titania and King Oberon, the rulers of Fairyland. The girls had worked with many of their fairy friends to outsmart Jack Frost and his tricky goblins. Most of all, they had kept the fairies a secret — if other humans found out about Fairyland, fairy magic would be in great danger.

"I'll tell you one thing we could have planned better," Mrs. Tate said after a moment. "The weather."

It was true. It was supposed to be a Fall Festival, but it felt more like the peak of summer! The sun was blazing hot. It was a perfect day for swimming, but the pools had been closed for two months!

It seemed like it was getting even hotter. The weather forecasters couldn't explain it.

"You can't plan the weather, I guess," Rachel said with a laugh, but Mrs. Tate just shook her head.

"I hope the heat won't keep people away from the festival," Mrs. Tate worried out loud. "Kyra's worked so hard to make it perfect."

"Look! We're almost there," Kirsty called out. "Just around this bend."

But as the farm came into view, Kirsty gasped. All the plants in the field looked dry and wilted. As they drove by, the girls could see piles of rotten fruit on the ground.

"It doesn't look like I expected,"
Rachel said before she could stop herself.

"No," Kirsty agreed. "Something is
terribly wrong." She looked out at the
dry fields. The cows couldn't even find
any grass to nibble on! She knew how
much the weather affected farms, but

Kyra's farm had been thriving a week ago. Now it was a mess. Something wasn't right.

"I can't believe I'm saying this," Kirsty whispered to her best friend, "but I hope Jack Frost is up to his old tricks."

"Kirsty!" Rachel exclaimed in a hushed voice. "How could you hope that Jack Frost is causing trouble on the farm?"

"That's not exactly what I meant," Kirsty replied. "I just know something is wrong. I feel awful about what's happening here. But if it's Jack Frost's fault, we can do something about it."

Mrs. Tate was mumbling in the front seat. "It's probably this awful heat. Or maybe there are beetles attacking all the plants," she said to herself. She shook her head as she turned the car onto the farm's long dirt driveway.

Rachel thought about what Kirsty and her mom had said. If it was the weather or some kind of bug, there was no way the girls could fix that. But if it was nasty Jack Frost, Rachel and Kirsty knew just what to do!

Squash Blossom Surprise

As soon as the engine stopped, Kirsty hopped out of the car. "Come on, Rachel!" she called. "Let's see how we can help!"

Rachel was at her friend's side at once. They could definitely help with the farmyard chores, but they might be able to do even more. "Let's look for signs of

Jack Frost and his no-good goblins," she whispered. Kirsty smiled, happy they had the same plan.

"Hey!" a voice called. Rachel looked up to see a tall woman in lace-up work boots taking long strides toward them. "You guys are real troopers, coming out in this heat," the woman said. She had a long blond braid down her back and crystal-blue eyes. "You must be Rachel."

Rachel returned her smile. "Yes. I'm visiting Kirsty for the festival. We're here to volunteer, if you need help getting ready."

"Yes, indeed," the farmer said. "I can't thank you enough. Suddenly, there's a ton of work to do around here. I'm not sure what's going on."

Rachel, Kirsty, and Mrs. Tate listened with concern. "Early this week, as the temperature got hotter, the fruit began to rot and the crops drooped," Kyra explained. "I can't seem to water them enough."

"Could it be some kind of bug?" Mrs. Tate asked.

Kirsty was wondering the same thing. She kept hearing a loud buzzing sound. She noticed that Rachel was looking around, too. Did she hear the same thing?

Just then, the buzzing became clearer. It was a whisper!

"Rachel, Kirsty! Look down!" the whisper said.

The girls locked eyes, then quickly dropped their gazes. They looked around the area near their feet.

There, hidden under the yellow petals of a squash blossom, was a tiny fairy!

She was waving
her arms up at
the girls.

Kirsty quickly
shifted her feet so
that she was shielding the fairy from
view. When her mom gave her a funny
look, Kirsty put on a grin and pretended
to listen to the adults' conversation.

"Come over here and look at the
corn," Kyra said to Mrs. Tate.

As soon as the adults were behind the tall cornstalks, Rachel and Kirsty kneeled down.

"Hello!" they both said.

"Hello, Rachel and Kirsty!" the fairy said as she stepped onto the blossom's stem. She was dressed in deep plum, golden yellow, and orange, with brown boots and long reddish-brown hair. She wiped teeny beads of sweat from her nose. "Excuse me," she said with a sigh.

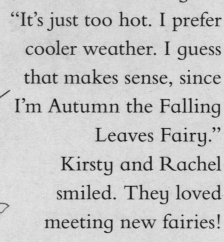

"It's just too hot. I prefer cooler weather. I guess that makes sense, since I'm Autumn the Falling Leaves Fairy." Kirsty and Rachel smiled. They loved meeting new fairies!

"The only problem is, unless you help me, there may not be any falling leaves this year," Autumn said, shaking her head. "In fact, there may not be any fall at all!"

"Oh, no!" Kirsty exclaimed. "No fall? Does it have anything to do with this strange heat wave?"

"It has everything to do with the heat," Autumn answered. "It's a long story, but it starts with Jack Frost."

Rachel and Kirsty weren't surprised. Jack Frost was *always* causing trouble! They listened closely to Autumn.

"I'm sure you know that Jack Frost loves winter. The freezing-cold weather fits his icy

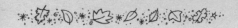

personality," Autumn explained. "This year, he couldn't wait for the cold weather, so he decided to try to trick nature and skip fall altogether."

"He wanted to go straight from summer to winter?" Kirsty asked, making sure she understood.

"Exactly," said Autumn. "And he knew just how to do it."

Endless Summer?

"What did Jack Frost do this time?"
Rachel wondered out loud.

"He stole my three magical objects that
get the fall season started," Autumn
answered. "He was very clever. I didn't
even realize that they were gone right
away!" Autumn went on to list the three
objects. She explained that the first, a

scarf, brought the brisk breezes that were the first sign of fall. The second, a pumpkin, made the fall harvest extra magical. The third object was a beautiful ruby-red leaf. The leaf told the trees that it was time for their leaves to change color and fall to the ground.

Rachel looked around. The leaves were still all green and on the trees.

"When summer was almost over," Autumn continued, "I went to get my three objects out of their hiding place. I always keep them in an old hatbox in my closet. But this time, they were gone!"

"If Jack Frost stole your objects," Kirsty

thought out loud, "why isn't it winter now?"

"Because that's not the way nature works," Autumn told the girls. "The seasons follow a cycle. Summer leads to fall. Fall leads to winter, and so on. It isn't natural to skip a season." The fairy sighed again.

"So Jack Frost messed up the cycle," Rachel reasoned.

"Yes, and now we're stuck in summer until we can find my magical objects," explained Autumn. "The one good thing is that Jack Frost didn't want anyone to know he had the objects, so he hid them with a magical spell. I know that they are somewhere nearby. Now that I'm

close, the goblins are trying to find them, too." She sighed. "If they get the objects, Jack Frost will hide them all over again."

"Not if we stop him!" Rachel said.

Kirsty put her hands on her hips. "We've never let him win, and we're not going to start now."

Autumn nodded in agreement. "Then let's get to work," she declared. "But first, I have to take off this jacket! I'm so hot, I can barely think!" The fairy *was* wearing an awful lot of layers. Kirsty could tell she was too warm.

Autumn took off her jacket, and Kirsty tucked it into her pocket. "Let's hope you

need this later," she said.
Then the girls quickly
asked Kyra for a chore
that they could do
around the farm.

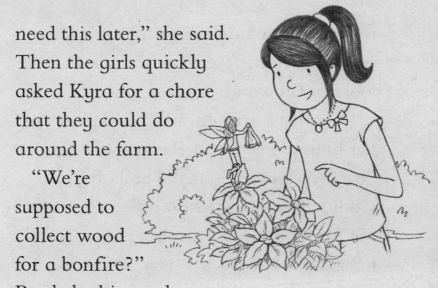

"We're
supposed to
collect wood
for a bonfire?"
Rachel whispered to
Kirsty after they had talked to the
farmer. "It's hard to get excited about a
bonfire in this heat."

Kirsty could see Rachel's
point. "Well, the Fall
Festival is supposed to
open with a really big
bonfire," she said.
"There will be

marshmallows and ghost stories." Kirsty sighed. "We can't let Kyra down. Let's look for firewood `and the goblins."

"And my scarf," Autumn added from her hiding spot under Rachel's ponytail. "It's a very pretty scarf. The Fairy Godmother knit it just for me. She looks out for all of us in Fairyland and I'll feel terrible if I can't get it back."

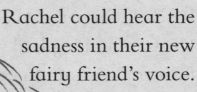

Rachel could hear the sadness in their new fairy friend's voice. There wasn't much to be happy about right now. The girls could see signs of trouble all over the

farm. The workers were rushing around, trying to deal with the thirsty animals and the weary crops. But this was just one farm. The extra-long, extra-hot summer would hurt the farms and the forests everywhere. It would be horrible!

Scarf Snatcher!

"I know!" Kirsty burst out after they had been collecting wood for a while. "Let's go down to the pond. There's lots of shade there." With the heat, both girls were already exhausted, and the wheelbarrow wasn't even half full.

As Rachel pushed the wheelbarrow, Autumn flew over and perched on it.

"Girls, one thing to know is that my scarf can make a small area cool, even on a hot day," the fairy said. "The real magic only happens when I wear it. When I put it on, the cool breezes flow everywhere and fall can begin."

The girls couldn't wait for that to happen!

Soon, the pond came into view.
"It's so pretty," Rachel said,
lowering the
wheelbarrow.
They could
see a wooden
dock with a
rowboat,
lily pads,
and a
waterfall at
one end. A
few low
quacks came
from a family
of ducks resting
in the shade
of a tree.

"They must be too hot," Kirsty

guessed. "The ducks usually swim around those cattails." She pointed to the other side of the pond, then frowned. "That's funny. Do you see that silvery glow over there?"

Both Autumn and Rachel gazed across the pond. "It looks like frost!" Autumn cried. "That means it's chilly. My scarf must be there!" Autumn spun into the air with excitement, then looked at the girls. "Quick! I'll change you into fairies so we can fly over the pond."

"Oh, yes!" the girls exclaimed together.

With three whisks of her wand, Autumn cast her spell. Orange and gold glitter swirled around the girls. In a moment, they had both shrunk to fairy-size and had delicate wings on their backs. They took to the air and glided toward the pond.

"I can sense that my scarf is close," Autumn said. Rachel scanned the area around the cattails for the hand-knit scarf. "Oh, no!" she grumbled. "I spy a goblin!"

Autumn and Kirsty looked at where Rachel was pointing. "There are lots of them!" Kirsty exclaimed with a gasp.

"But only one has my scarf," Autumn declared, zooming ahead.

The girls flew after her.

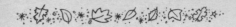

The one goblin was racing away from the others. "I found the scarf! I found the scarf!" he chanted as he ran. A lovely, long orange-and-white-striped scarf was wrapped around his neck.

The other goblins were soon sweating and panting. They couldn't keep up! The goblin with the scarf ran all the way

around the pond, still feeling nice and
cool. He quickly looked behind him and
then jumped into the
rowboat. "What
a nice, brisk
day for a boat
ride," he
mumbled,
pleased that he
had outrun his friends. . . .

But he had not outrun the fairies!

"Not so fast!" Autumn yelled as the
goblin pushed the boat into the pond.

"What?" the goblin screeched.
"Fairies?"

"You'd better believe it!" Autumn said
as Kirsty and Rachel flew up behind her.

"There's no way you can beat me in
this heat," the goblin said with a laugh.

He grabbed the paddles and rowed to the
center of the pond. The fairies just
watched him, trying to catch their
breath.

"Now what do we do?" Rachel asked.

"I need to take a break," Kirsty
confessed.

"That's right," Autumn said. "We take
a break . . . and make a plan."

Rachel and Kirsty had a special talent
for making plans. They had often tricked
the goblins in the past. But as the three
friends sat on a tree branch, they couldn't
think of a thing to do.

"It's just so hot," Kirsty
said.

"I don't have any
energy to think,"
Rachel agreed.

"I don't have any energy to move," Autumn admitted. "I can't take the heat."

Just then, the other goblins stumbled around to the dock. They looked at the goblin with the scarf and grumbled.

"He's so selfish," one complained. "Why isn't he sharing?"

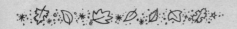

"We're sopping wet, and he's nice and cool in his boat," another grouched.

"I think he needs to be taught a lesson," the tallest goblin declared.

The three fairies watched with interest. "Let's see what they do," suggested Rachel. "Maybe *they* have a plan!"

A Plan at the Pond

Rachel, Kirsty, and Autumn watched the goblins from above. Chuckling to themselves, the silly green creatures gathered handfuls of acorns. Then they all walked out onto the skinny dock. The goblin with the scarf was leaning back in the boat, his eyes closed.

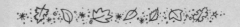

"Hey! What was that?" a big-footed goblin yelled.

"It looks like an alligator!" yelled another.

"A hungry alligator," the tallest goblin agreed.

Then they started to throw acorns into the pond, close to the rowboat.

The three fairies watched silently.

An acorn landed close to the boat and splashed the goblin with the scarf in the face. "Hey, what was that?" he grunted.

"Look out," a goblin on the dock yelled. "There's an alligator!"

"What?" cried the goblin in the boat. He grabbed on to both sides of the scarf and clung to it in fear. He stared into the dark water. There was a splash on the other side of the boat. "Whoa! Help me!" he cried. "An alligator would love to eat me. I'd be so tasty!" He scrambled around in the boat, trying to reach the

oars, but he accidentally knocked them
both in the water.

"You're in the pond without a paddle!"
one of the goblins on the dock yelled.

"How am I going to get back?" the
goblin screeched in a panic. He was
stuck!

"You can ride on the back of the
alligator!" the big-footed goblin cackled.

All the goblins burst out laughing.

"Help me!" the goblin in the boat
cried, chewing on the end of the scarf in
fear.

"Oh, that's just disgusting," Autumn
declared under
her breath. She
covered her eyes.

"Don't worry,"
Kirsty reassured

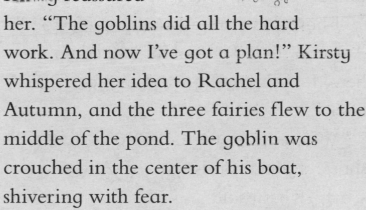

her. "The goblins did all the hard
work. And now I've got a plan!" Kirsty
whispered her idea to Rachel and
Autumn, and the three fairies flew to the
middle of the pond. The goblin was
crouched in the center of his boat,
shivering with fear.

"Are you in trouble?" Rachel asked,
fluttering just above the rowboat.

"I'm scared," the goblin confessed.

"Yeah," Kirsty said with wide eyes. "We heard something about an alligator."

"A huge alligator with teeth like knives," the goblin said. "I don't want to be his dinner! I really, really don't want that."

"I have something I really want, too," Autumn said. The goblin looked up at her. "I really, really want my scarf back."

"We can promise to get you safely to shore, if you promise to give Autumn her scarf," Kirsty said.

The goblin looked at the dock, where all the other goblins were laughing. He

frowned, still scanning
the water for the
alligator.

Out of the corner of
her eye, Rachel saw a
frog jump into the
pond with a loud
splash.

"Yikes!" the goblin
yelled. "It's the alligator!" He quickly
unwrapped the scarf and threw it at
Autumn. She swooped down to catch it
just before it dropped in the pond.

"Thank you!" she exclaimed.

As soon as she grabbed the scarf, it
shrunk to fairy-size. With an elegant
swish, Autumn tossed the scarf around
her neck. A brisk breeze instantly swept
across the pond, making it easier for the

three tiny fairies to tow the rowboat
ashore.

At once, Kirsty noticed the rustle of the
wind in the trees. Rachel felt a delightful
shiver as a rush of air lifted the hair off
her neck. The scarf was working its
magic!

"We don't have a moment to spare,"

Autumn said. "I'll change you back to girls and make sure you have plenty of firewood. The Fall Festival is about to begin!"

In no time at all, glitter circled around the girls and they grew to their full size. When they looked at the wheelbarrow, it was full of neatly stacked sticks.

"I can't thank you enough," Autumn said as she evened out the cozy scarf around her neck. "Luckily, I'll get another chance tomorrow! For now, I have to head back to Fairyland to share the good news."

Another swirl of gold and orange glitter whooshed into the air, and Autumn vanished.

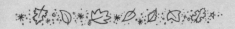

"Brrr," Kirsty said, lifting the wheelbarrow handles. As the girls headed toward the barnyard in search of Kyra and Mrs. Tate, the air grew even cooler. "I'm glad we packed warmer clothes in the car trunk. We'll have to change before the bonfire."

Rachel rubbed her arms to stay warm and smiled at her friend. "I think fall really has begun," she said. "And so has another fairy adventure!"

A Plump
Pumpkin

Contents

An Early Start

When Kirsty Tate woke up the next
morning, her nose was cold. A crisp
breeze lifted the curtains from the
window, and a sliver of sunlight
brightened the room. Her best friend,
Rachel Walker, snuggled under her
blankets as she blinked awake.

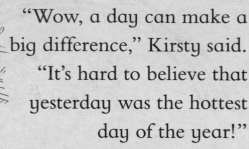

"Wow, a day can make a big difference," Kirsty said. "It's hard to believe that yesterday was the hottest day of the year!"

"Today feels chilly," Rachel agreed. "Just like a fall morning should be." Thanks to Kirsty and Rachel, Autumn the Falling Leaves Fairy had her beautiful magic scarf back from Jack Frost's goblins! As soon as Autumn had placed it around her neck, the brisk breezes of fall had chased the heat away. By the time the Fall Festival opened with a big bonfire, it had felt like fall. Lots of people showed up and toasted marshmallows, crowding around the fire to stay warm in the night chill.

But Jack Frost and his goblins still had

two of Autumn's magic objects, and Rachel and Kirsty were determined to get them back. The success of the Fall Festival at New Growth Farm depended on it!

Of course, both girls understood that the problem was bigger than the Fall Festival. Kyra, the farmer, needed a good harvest so she would have enough money to keep the farm going over the winter. Plus, autumn *everywhere* was a mess, not just in Kirsty's town!

"Why are we still in bed?" Rachel asked suddenly. "We have a ton to do today!"

"I know," Kirsty said with a nervous sigh. The girls got

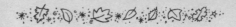

dressed, putting on lots of layers in order
to stay toasty, and
raced down the
stairs. Mrs. Tate
was sitting at the
kitchen table,
shaking her head.
"What is it, Mom?"
Kirsty asked.

"The newspaper says that all the local
farmers are having trouble," Mrs. Tate
explained. "Just like Kyra. Some crops
are getting ripe too fast and rotting.
Others aren't growing at all."

"That's horrible," Rachel said out loud.
She couldn't help thinking about how it
was all Jack Frost's fault. He should never
have stolen the magic objects! Autumn's
magic pumpkin had the power to protect

the fall harvest. Rachel and Kirsty had to find that pumpkin, even if it took all day!

"We should go straight to New Growth Farm," Kirsty said. She grabbed her lunch bag and stuffed some muffins and other snacks inside. "We're ready!"

Mrs. Tate looked surprised. "You don't want to sit down and eat?" she asked. "You should take it easy. We were at the bonfire very late last night."

"We want to help Kyra," Kirsty insisted. She looked at Rachel, who nodded.

"Well, OK," Mrs. Tate said, gathering

her breakfast dishes. "I'll leave a note for your dad. He can join us later."

Kirsty and Rachel rushed out to the car. They both knew what they had to do! The farm was a big place. Finding one small pumpkin wouldn't be easy, especially when the goblins would also be looking for it.

They spotted Kyra as soon as Mrs. Tate pulled into the long driveway. The farmer was feeding the chickens. After she closed the car door, Kirsty looked around at the large fields filled with all kinds of greens and vegetables. As expected, nothing looked ready to harvest—and worse, some of the plants looked rotten! The tomatoes had brown bottoms, and the apples were full of worms. The girls would have to work fast if they wanted to find the pumpkin before the festival opened again at noon.

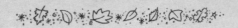

"We have to decide where to start," Kirsty whispered as they followed her mom toward the chicken pen.

"Yes," Rachel agreed. "We need a strategy." She shook her head as they passed by a patch of droopy lettuce. "A very good strategy."

A Stuffy Fairy

"I need two wheelbarrows of gourds," Kyra said to Kirsty and Rachel after everyone had said hello. "Can you pick them for me?"

The girls gave Kyra blank stares.

"You know what gourds are, don't you?" Kyra smiled. "The gourd is a plant family that includes squash, melons, and pumpkins," she explained. "We'll put the gourds in special gift baskets. The baskets will be the prizes for our games today."

"That sounds great!" Kirsty enthused. She gave Kyra a big smile. Then she and Rachel each took the handles of a wheelbarrow and started to roll them away. But as soon as Kyra had disappeared inside the farmhouse, Kirsty's smile disappeared, too. "Two wheelbarrows?" she asked, trying to balance her wheelbarrow with its extra-wide handles. "How are we going to fill two? We'll be lucky to fill one." She knew what a gourd was, but she *didn't* know how they would find that many ripe ones.

"I know. When we saw them yesterday, all the squash were too small to pick," Rachel agreed. "We'd better get started."

"Let's look for Autumn's magic pumpkin at the same time," Kirsty suggested.

"That's perfect, because a pumpkin is a gourd," Rachel reminded her friend.

"Leafy greens are planted in this part of the field," Kirsty explained with a smile. "We should head over toward the apple orchard. The gourds are over there."

Rachel shielded her eyes from the sun so she could see the other side of the field. "Let's hope the magic pumpkin is hidden with the other gourds."

Just then, the girls heard a small sneeze. And another. And then a sniff. "Excuse me," said a tiny voice.

"Autumn, is that you?" Rachel asked uncertainly. It didn't sound like their new fairy friend.

"Yes, it is! I'm down here," said the voice.

Rachel and Kirsty crouched down and saw Autumn. She was sitting on a kale leaf and held a handkerchief in her hand. Her eyes were puffy, and her nose was a rosy red.

"Oh, Autumn! Have you been crying?" Kirsty asked.

"No," Autumn said. "I have a cold. My eyes won't stop watering." She took a deep breath and blew her nose. Her entire body seemed to shake. "I feel like I *could* cry, though," she added. "This farm makes me so sad. None of the plants are growing like they should."

"We have to find your magic pumpkin," Rachel said. "It's the only way to make things right. But how will we find one pumpkin in the middle of a huge farm?"

"There's a special trick," Autumn said in a small voice. "You know that my pumpkin's magic brings a healthy fall harvest. It also helps remind people of the wonderful foods that come from fresh farm crops."

"How does it do that?" Rachel wondered.

"It smells like warm pumpkin bread, right from the oven!" Autumn said. The very thought made the fairy smile, and her nose crinkled.

"Oh, that sounds wonderful," Kirsty said.

"The trouble is that I can't smell anything," Autumn said with a sniff. "This cold is so bad I can hardly breathe.

Without my special objects, I don't have all my powers. I can't even make myself better."

Rachel's eyes filled with concern. She hated being sick! It was especially hard if there was something important that you had to do. "Don't worry, Autumn. Kirsty and I will help you find the pumpkin."

"My mom says I have a great sense of smell," Kirsty added. "Let's put that nose to work," Autumn said with a giggle— then she sneezed.

A Pretty Pumpkin

The morning air was still cool, so Rachel and Kirsty were happy to keep moving. As they bent down to check for gourds, the sun felt warm on the backs of their heads. "This is slow work," Kirsty said, lifting a large leaf away from a prickly vine. She looked under it, but she saw only the ground.

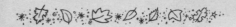

"It's taking a long time because there aren't very many gourds," Autumn said. Rachel sighed. There were only four yellow squash in her wheelbarrow. Kirsty had three honeydew melons and two zucchini.

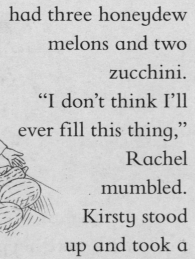

"I don't think I'll ever fill this thing," Rachel mumbled. Kirsty stood up and took a deep breath. "I smell something," Kirsty said, her eyes open wide. "I think it smells like something baking, but I can't tell where it's coming from." She turned around and sniffed again. "It always smells like it's right behind me."

"Does it smell like pumpkin bread?" Autumn asked, biting her lip. "Like cinnamon?"

"I don't know," Kirsty said. "I think I might smell chocolate?"

Autumn looked puzzled.

"Um, Kirsty?" Rachel began. "Doesn't your mom put chocolate chips in her special muffins?"

"When I'm lucky!" Kirsty said with a laugh.

"Isn't that what she made this morning?" Rachel asked.

Kirsty nodded.

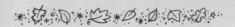

"And didn't you pack some muffins in your backpack?" Rachel added.

Kirsty blushed. "Well, that explains why the smell is always behind me," she said with a giggle. "Would anyone like a muffin?" The girls and Autumn sat down in the rough grass at the edge of the field. Kirsty opened the foil wrap and handed a muffin to Rachel. She tore off a little crumb and passed it to Autumn, who held it in both hands.

As they ate, the breeze shifted. It was now coming across the field, brushing over the tall cornstalks.

"Wait," Kirsty said. "I think I smell something new." She lifted her nose slightly and took in short breaths of air. "Autumn, I smell cinnamon now. And warm, rich pumpkin!"

"Oh!" Autumn cried. She popped the rest of the muffin in her mouth and clapped for joy. "Quick, we have to find it. Leave your things in the wheelbwarrow, and I'll turn you into fairies. We'll see things so much

better if we can glide over the fields."

"Now I can smell it, too!" Rachel announced. "It smells delicious!" Both girls stood still as Autumn swirled her wand. Deep orange and gold fairy dust whipped through the air and circled the two friends. Their feet gently left the ground, and soon wings appeared on their backs. Rachel and Kirsty smiled at each other. It was so much fun being fairies!

Once they had shrunk to Autumn's size, Rachel and Kirsty flew into the air

behind their newest fairy friend. They
needed to flap their wings hard because
they were going against the wind. But
the smell of yummy pumpkin bread grew
stronger, and it encouraged them to keep
going.

"I see something up ahead," Autumn

yelled over the wind. "It looks like there's a big space in the middle of the corn. Maybe the pumpkin is down there."

Kirsty scanned the field. She could see it, too. There was a bare spot where no corn was growing.

The three friends held their breath as they flew over the spot. Then Rachel gasped. There was a gorgeous orange pumpkin below them! It was a little bigger than a basketball, and nice and plump. Rachel was sure the wonderful smell was coming from this giant gourd.

There was just one problem: A goblin was sitting smack-dab on top of it.

A Helping Paw

"Is that your pumpkin?" Rachel asked Autumn.

Autumn nodded.

"At least we know where it is now," Kirsty said. She was trying to look on the bright side of things.

The three fairies hovered over the scene. There was one goblin sitting on the pumpkin, and three other goblins standing nearby among the cornstalks.

"They're guarding it," Kirsty said to her friends.

"How long do I have to sit here?" the first goblin yelled. "My rump is getting sore." The other goblins snorted and covered their mouths.

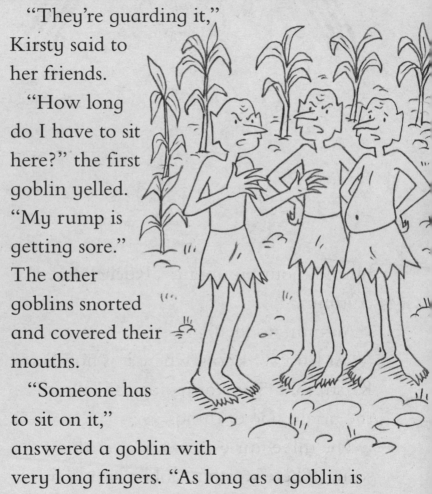

"Someone has to sit on it," answered a goblin with very long fingers. "As long as a goblin is

touching it, a fairy can't shrink it down
to its magic size."

"Why me?" asked the first goblin.
His voice was high
and whiny.
"Because you're
good at it," said
the long-fingered
goblin. "Besides,
the rest of us are
hungry. We're going
to find something
to eat."

"I want that
pumpkin bread
we smell. Let's
find it," a pot-bellied
goblin suggested. "I could eat a whole
loaf."

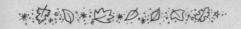

When the fairies heard this, they laughed a little, too. "The goblins don't realize that the smell is coming from my pumpkin," Autumn said. "There isn't any pumpkin bread yet, because there aren't any ripe pumpkins."

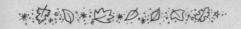

"Don't you get up!" The goblin pointed his long finger when he spoke. "Or Jack Frost will be mad at you."

"But I'm hungry, too," the whiny goblin mumbled. He frowned as the other goblins walked away.

Rachel motioned to Kirsty and Autumn. "Let's talk somewhere else. We don't want him to hear us," she whispered. The three fairies flew to

another part of the cornfield. They all
perched on a stalk.

"How are we going to get the
pumpkin?" Autumn asked. "We can't just
pull it out from under him, and it won't
shrink to fairy-size if he's sitting on it."

"We just need to get him to stand up,"
said Rachel.

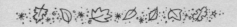

"Let's think," Kirsty said.

All at once, their cornstalk started to shake. "What was that?" Rachel asked. She grabbed on to a tiny ear of corn. Kirsty clung to the stalk. But Autumn just fluttered her wings and floated to the ground.

"Well, hello!" Autumn exclaimed. Kirsty and Rachel looked down and saw a fuzzy brown groundhog next to Autumn. He was standing on his hind legs. "He must have been shaking the cornstalk," Kirsty said.

"Were you trying to get our attention?" Autumn asked.

The groundhog nodded. Then he let out a series of chirps, high and low.

"I see. You know about Jack Frost," Autumn said. "And you want to help us?"

The groundhog blinked his sparkly eyes and nodded again.

Kirsty and Rachel looked at each other, amazed. Autumn understood the groundhog! The girls flew down. Soon, other animals joined their group. The rabbits, chipmunks, and birds wanted to help, too. There were

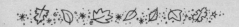

lots of squeaks and chirps and tweets.

Of course—Jack Frost has made life hard on the animals, too, Kirsty realized. *They don't have food, either. The acorns aren't even falling from the oak trees.*

They all started to think of a plan.

"First, we need the goblin to get off the pumpkin," Rachel said. "Second, Autumn has to touch the pumpkin. Then it will shrink, and the harvest magic can happen."

They all agreed that they couldn't let the goblin see the fairies. "If he knows we're nearby, he won't get off the pumpkin," Autumn said.

"He might see us if we fly," Kirsty added. "We'll have to find another way."

Just then, the groundhog started chirping. He looked at the rabbits and the chipmunks. They squeaked a willing reply. Autumn nodded slowly, and her face broke into a huge grin.

Together, the fairies and their friends came up with the perfect pumpkin plan!

Underground Gourd!

A little while later, the rabbits,
chipmunks, and groundhog crawled
out of a hole.

"Wow! Are you done?" Autumn asked.
"That was a lot of work."

The groundhog made a light grunt,
and then he nudged Autumn's shoulder
with his wet nose.

87

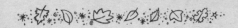

"Stop it," she said with a giggle. "That tickles!"

Kirsty and Rachel both gave the rabbits and chipmunks long pats. "Thank you," they said to their new friends.

"It's our turn, girls," Autumn said. She gave her nose one last blow and then lifted her wand.

"Are you ready?" Kirsty called to the birds in the trees. "Here's the pumpkin bread!" Moments before, Autumn had used her magic to make one slice of pumpkin bread. It was wrapped in a red-and-white napkin, and it smelled delicious. The blue jay swooped down and grabbed the bread with its feet. Then it took off over the cornfield with the other birds.

"Good luck!" Kirsty called.

"I hope this works," Rachel said with a sigh.

The animals had dug a tunnel that was just wide enough for the fairies to fit through. The fairies had to crawl—there wasn't enough room to flap their wings. Autumn used her wand like a flashlight so they could see.

"I wonder how far we'll have to go," Rachel said.

"We'll know when we're close," Autumn said. "We'll hear the birds. Let's hope they can trick the goblin."

They crawled for a few more minutes, and then they suddenly heard a ruckus.

"Hey! I smell more pumpkin bread. You greedy bird, give it to me!" the goblin yelled.

Kirsty could picture the goblin yelling at the birds. She guessed that the blue jay was flying just out of his reach. The first part of their plan was working!

"This is where the tunnel ends," Autumn said.

"I can see the bottom of the pumpkin!" Rachel pointed at a patch of orange poking through the tunnel exit. Just above them, the goblin was sitting on the pumpkin.

"As soon as he gets up, I'll touch it," Autumn said.

"Here's the peephole!" Rachel pointed

to a small gap in the tunnel roof. She and Kirsty climbed up and carefully looked out.

"You silly birds! Give it to me. I want that treat!" the girls heard the goblin whine. "I'll get up just for a minute. No one will know."

Kirsty and Rachel watched through the peephole. They saw two big green feet. The feet were running away from the pumpkin!

"He stood up!"
Kirsty yelled.
As soon as
Autumn touched
the pumpkin, it
began to shrink.

Soon, it was small enough to fit in
Autumn's hands.

Rachel stuck her head out of the hole.
The birds were flying away, but the
goblin was busy gobbling up the
pumpkin bread. "He doesn't
know we have the pumpkin,"
she said. "Hurry,
let's go!"

The three fairies flew
out of the tunnel and into
the air. They rushed back to
their meeting place so they could

celebrate with the animals and the birds. Their plan had worked!

The farm began to change at once. The corn ears grew larger, the pumpkins plumped up, and the tomatoes turned a deep, ripe red. Suddenly, the greens all looked fresh and healthy.

"Nature really is amazing!" Kirsty exclaimed as she scratched one of the rabbits behind his ears.

"It's the real magic," Autumn agreed. "Today, I'm giving nature a little help." Autumn waved her wand, and picture-perfect apples magically dropped from the trees into baskets, without a bump or bruise! "And I think 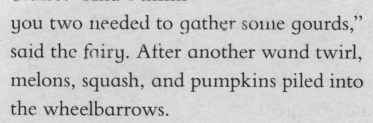 you two needed to gather some gourds," said the fairy. After another wand twirl, melons, squash, and pumpkins piled into the wheelbarrows.

"I can't wait to show Kyra all these gourds!" Rachel said.

"We need to get these to her so they

can go in the gift baskets," Kirsty agreed. "Then we can play games and eat some of the fall foods."

"Before I head back to Fairyland, I'll make sure to fill the refreshment table with pumpkin bread, pear pie, zucchini muffins, and apple cider," Autumn promised.

Kirsty heard her stomach rumble. "Thank you so much, Autumn," she said. "You saved the farm's Fall Festival."

"I couldn't have done it without your help," the fairy insisted. "We make a great team!" With a whisk of her wand, she

changed Kirsty and Rachel into girls again. Then she winked, circled herself with fairy dust, and vanished. Only the smell of cinnamon remained.

"We have one more magic object to find," Rachel said, turning to Kirsty with a grin.

"And one more day together to do it," added Kirsty. "Until then, we can have fun at the Fall Festival!"

"I, for one, am hungry for pumpkin bread," Rachel said. With that, the two friends headed for the food tables, hand in hand.

A Leaf of
Ruby Red

Contents

The Last Day

"I can't believe all the leaves are still green," Kirsty Tate said to her best friend, Rachel Walker. "The hills are usually a mix of orange, red, yellow, and even purple by now."

Rachel looked at the trees around New Growth Farm. From the rows of apple trees in the orchard to the maple and oak

trees in the forest, all the leaves were bright green. Rachel shook her head. She

knew what was going on. "It's all because of Jack Frost. He stole Autumn's ruby-red leaf. That's why the forest is not full of color." Rachel and Kirsty had already helped their new friend, Autumn the Falling Leaves Fairy, find two of her missing objects. Thanks to them, the weather had turned cool and crisp, and the fall crops were ripe and ready for harvest. The last missing object was a ruby-red leaf. Once Autumn and the girls found it, the trees would know it was fall. Then the leaves would change color and drop to the ground.

"I hope we can find the missing leaf before this afternoon," Kirsty said.

"I know," Rachel agreed. "The Leaf Leap is supposed to start at three o'clock, right?"

Kirsty nodded. It was the last day of the Fall Festival at New Growth Farm. Kirsty and Rachel were at the farm early to help get ready. There were lots of great events planned for the day, but the highlight was the Great Leaf Leap. After the kids and adults raked the leaves into a giant pile, they could take turns jumping into it from a wooden platform!

Today, Rachel and Kirsty's job was to start the leaf pile. They had work gloves, rakes, and leaf bags. They even had warm apple cider to drink during their break—but they didn't have any leaves!

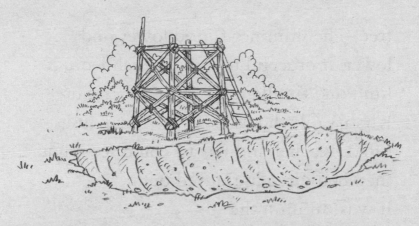

Rachel looked up at the wooden platform. Then she looked down into the gully where they were supposed to jump. "It would take truckloads of leaves to fill the gully," Rachel said with concern. "It has to be nice and soft for a safe landing."

"What seems to be the problem?" asked a silvery voice. It sounded far away. Both girls searched for the voice's owner. Finally, they saw a red shimmer, high in the branches of an old maple tree. The shimmer flitted lower and lower. It gracefully dodged each leafy limb and finally landed on the end of Kirsty's rake handle. As the fairy dust lifted, Rachel and Kirsty could see what they had already figured out: It was Autumn the Falling Leaves Fairy! She was wearing her magical scarf—the one that brought the brisk fall breezes—and a great big smile.

The girls quickly brought their fairy friend up to date. "Autumn, we need to find your magical leaf," said Kirsty. "It's the only way we'll have enough leaves to fill the gully."

"Let's start looking for it! My leaf is

such a bright red that we should be able
to spot it right away if it's here at the
farm," Autumn explained.

Autumn and the girls took a quick tour
of the farm. All the leaves were still a
fresh summery green.

"I see red tomatoes
and red apples, but
no red leaves," Rachel
said.

"If you were Jack
Frost, where would
you hide a leaf?"
Autumn asked.

They all frowned in thought.

"I've got it!" Kirsty cried. "Let's look in
the forest!"

"Of course!" Autumn exclaimed.
"We'll get there faster if we all can fly.

Would you like to be fairies?"

"Oh, yes," the girls replied together.

Autumn twirled her wand. Orange and gold glitter swirled around the girls. Their bodies began to shrink, and sparkly wings began to grow on their backs. Soon, they were fairies, just like Autumn! They flapped their wings and rose into the air.

"Remember, the goblins might have found my leaf already," Autumn said.

"We'll keep an eye out for them, too," Kirsty said as they flew over the cornfield.

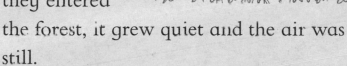

As soon as they entered the forest, it grew quiet and the air was still.

"Why aren't the birds chirping?" Rachel wondered.

"Something weird is going on," Autumn agreed. "We just have to find out what it is."

Whispers in the Woods

Kirsty shivered. The woods seemed especially spooky. All the lush green leaves blocked out the sun. The fairies flew through the shadows. "Did you hear that?" Kirsty asked.

Pssssh, psssh, psssh.

"It sounds like the wind," Rachel said.

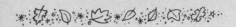

"But the leaves aren't moving," Kirsty pointed out.

The three fairies landed on a tree branch so they could listen more closely.

"I think someone is whispering," Autumn said, her own voice hushed.

"And I'll bet I know who it is," Rachel said quietly.

Autumn pointed up, and the girls understood at once. They all flitted up through the leaves. Soon, they were above the trees.

"Let's see if we can find the goblins from up here," Autumn said. She continued to fly higher, and the girls followed. "Aha! Over there!" Autumn motioned with her wand.

At once, the girls could see what Autumn had noticed. There was one tree that had its full fall colors: warm, deep reds and bold, bright oranges in the middle of lots and lots of green.

"My leaf is working its magic on that

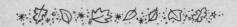

one tree!" Autumn exclaimed. The three
fairies began to fly toward the one
colorful tree. As they grew closer, the
whispers grew louder.

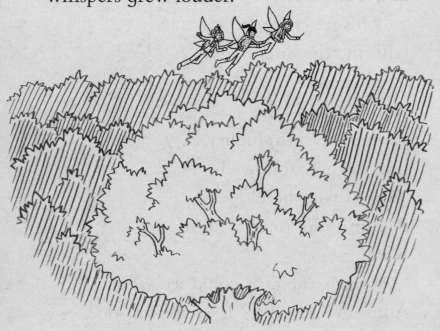

"Those are the loudest whispers I've
ever heard," said Rachel. "There must be
five or six goblins down there." The

fairies hovered above
the tree.

"It's beautiful," Kirsty said, looking
down. "But why do you think the
goblins are hanging out here?"

At once, Kirsty's question was
answered. A chilling crackle ripped
through the sky as an ice bolt wrapped
itself around the tree.

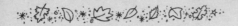

The fairies heard a horrible cackle that could only belong to one person: Jack Frost. Below, the beautiful tree was lost in a frosty blue fog.

"What happened?" Rachel asked, stunned.

When the fog lifted, the fairies understood. Jack Frost had used his icy magic. He had zapped the goblins back to his Ice Castle with him, and they had taken the magic leaf. "We have to follow them," Rachel insisted. "We can't let Jack Frost get away with this!"

"Don't worry," Autumn said, "we won't. But it isn't easy to beat Jack Frost in his own icy world. We need a plan, and I know who can help us come up with it."

Autumn led Kirsty and Rachel to a

stream that ran through the forest.
Between two fallen trees, there was a
spot where the stream was slow.

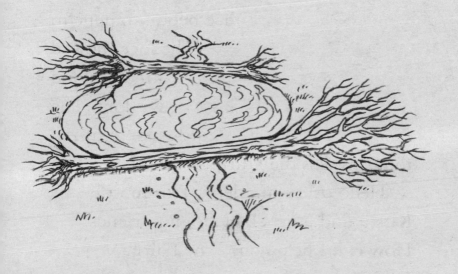

"We need to make a seeing pool,"
Autumn announced. "I think this water
is still enough." Rachel and Kirsty
watched, wondering what would
happen.

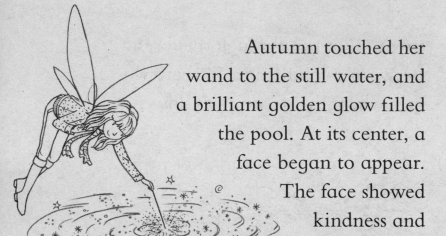

Autumn touched her wand to the still water, and a brilliant golden glow filled the pool. At its center, a face began to appear. The face showed kindness and wisdom. The girls soon realized that this was the Fairy Godmother.

"Hello, Autumn, dear. This must be Kirsty and Rachel. Hello, my friends. How can I help you?" the Fairy Godmother asked, her image shimmering in the magical pool.

Autumn quickly explained what had happened. "Can you help us think of a plan?"

The Fairy Godmother nodded. "If Jack

Frost takes the leaf into the Ice Castle, it will be hard to get out," she thought out loud. "His icy magic is very powerful there. It's good that you are wearing your magical scarf, Autumn. I think it could come in handy." The Fairy Godmother went on to explain how Autumn, Kirsty, and Rachel could get the leaf back—and give Jack Frost a taste of his own magic.

"That will be very tricky," Rachel said.

"And it could be dangerous," Autumn said.

"We'll help you, Autumn," Kirsty assured her friend.

"I know you can you do it," said the Fairy Godmother. "I wish you lots of luck. We're depending on you to get the seasons back to how they're supposed to be." The Fairy Godmother smiled, and the golden light disappeared from the stream.

The three fairies looked at one another. "Well, we know what we have to do," Rachel said. "Let's go do it!"

Autumn took a deep breath. "I wish there was another way. I don't want to use my scarf magic on the Ice Castle, but I'm ready if you are," she said. A dazzling stream of glitter burst from the wand's tip. It circled around the three tiny fairies, the wind whipping through their hair. Rachel and Kirsty could feel a tingling in their fingers and toes. Both girls closed their eyes. When they opened them, they were in Fairyland.

Hot on the Trail

"This is Fairyland Forest. Jack Frost's Ice Castle is right through these trees," Autumn explained.

Rachel and Kirsty looked for the silvery castle, but the trees were still too thick with green leaves.

"The seasons in Fairyland are still all messed up, too," Kirsty said.

"Yes, if the leaves don't change color and drop, we will always be stuck in summer," Autumn declared. "The human world will be, too."

Kirsty's eyes turned serious and she put her hands on her hips. She was about to say something, but she stopped. A troop of goblins was headed their way right now! *"Shhhhh!"* A harsh voice came from below. The *shush* was so loud, it echoed through the forest.

"If you make too much noise, the fairies will hear you," a goblin scolded.

"They still have the leaf!" Rachel
whispered to her friends. The goblins
were marching around with the bright
red leaf. The tallest goblin was waving
the leaf like a flag
in a parade.
Wherever they
went, the
magic leaf
brought fall
colors to the trees.

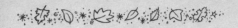

"Maybe we can stop them before they get to the Ice Castle," Kirsty said. "We can just swoop down and grab your leaf."

"It's worth a try," Autumn said.

"Then let's go," Kirsty announced, immediately diving toward the goblins. Rachel and Autumn followed right behind. Kirsty reached out for the leaf. Her fingers almost grasped it.

"Fairies!" the tallest goblin screeched when he saw her. "Run!" He swatted at Kirsty as he darted through the forest. Wherever he went, the leaves changed color and dropped. Now the leaf's magic was working too quickly. None of the leaves were turning red or orange. They all turned brown. The faster the goblin ran, the faster the leaves flew from the trees.

The falling leaves were as big as the fairies, and they filled the air. "I can't see!" yelled Rachel.

"It's like a blizzard of leaves," Autumn said. She watched as the trees shed all of their leaves at the same time. "This isn't how fall is supposed to be." She landed on a bare branch. "It shouldn't happen all at once." Her voice cracked as she

spoke. Kirsty and
Rachel perched
next to her.
Now that all the
leaves were on the
ground, the fairies had a clear view of
the Ice Castle. They could see the goblins
running toward Jack Frost's chilly home.
The land around the castle stayed slick
and snowy all year. Icicles
hung from the trees and
the castle roof. It
was a cold, scary
place.

"We have no
choice now,"
Autumn murmured.

Once the fairies had caught their
breath, they took off. As they flew

toward the Ice Castle, the air grew cold.
The wind was fierce, and it was hard
to fly.

"It's time for the plan," Autumn said.
"You find a way into the castle. I'll start
the scarf magic. I hope
the reverse spell works!"
Autumn flew over
the castle roof,
twirled her wand,
and began to chant.

"Magic scarf, this is the hour.
You must reverse your cooling power.
Make the harsh wind a nice, warm breeze,
So the ice can no longer freeze."

Autumn hoped the Fairy Godmother's
plan would work. She had used her
magic scarf to turn the wind from cold
to warm. The Falling Leaves Fairy

watched as the Ice Castle started to shine
with a wet glow. Drips fell from the roof
and balconies. Soon, streams of water
trickled out of the castle windows. "It's
started. I just hope I can stop it in time,"
Autumn whispered.

All Wet!

Rachel and Kirsty flew from window to window. Finally, they found one that was open a crack. Rachel looked in and gasped. "It's the throne room," she said. "There's Jack Frost."

"He has the leaf!" Kirsty declared. Jack Frost sat atop his icy throne. He

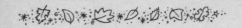

held the red leaf in his fist and smiled
smugly.

"Look, Autumn's spell is working. The
castle is melting," Rachel pointed out.
The girls stood on the windowsill and
watched. Tiny streams
of water flowed
down the walls
and pooled on the
Ice Castle's floor.
The goblins
began to splash
around in the
swiftly rising water.

"What are you doing?" Jack Frost
snapped at them. The water had not
reached his feet, but it was getting
higher.

"My toes are cold and wet!" a goblin

screeched as he climbed onto a table.

"It's melting," another goblin cried.
"The castle is melting!"

Jack Frost's head whipped around,
taking in the signs.

Just then, Autumn landed next to
Rachel and Kirsty.

"It's working, Autumn! You did it,"
said Rachel.

Autumn bit her lip. "It's working too well," she confessed. "We need to get the leaf soon. If too much of the castle melts, my magic won't be strong enough to fix it. All the melted water could flood Fairyland."

Just then, a gust of warm air rushed in from outside and pushed the three fairies inside the throne room. They flapped their wings and took flight. "Up here!" Kirsty called as she perched on a dripping chandelier.

"If the water gets high enough to distract Jack Fost, maybe we can just

grab the leaf from
him," Rachel
suggested.

"Maybe," Autumn
replied, "but I'm going
to try to reason with
him first. I know how
much the Ice Castle means to
him. I think he'll want to make a
trade—my leaf, for his home." The three
fairies looked below. The goblins were
all huddled together,
shivering on the large
banquet table. Jack Frost
stood defiantly on the
seat of his throne, his
mouth turned down
in an angry scowl.

"I'll need you for backup," Autumn
said. "Are you coming, girls?"

Rachel and Kirsty nodded. They all flew
down and hovered in front of Jack Frost.

"You!" Jack Frost scolded. "How dare
you melt my Ice Castle!"

"How dare you mix up the seasons!"
Autumn insisted.

"But this is my castle," Jack Frost said,
motioning with his arms. "The goblins
and I like it here. It's our home."

"But the human world is our home," Kirsty said.

"And Fairyland is our home," Autumn chimed in, looking Jack Frost in the eye. "It belongs to you, me, the goblins—all the Fairyland creatures. When you stole my magic objects, you messed with nature. We need to set things right. We need the seasons back so nature works the way it's supposed to again."

A large drip of melted ice fell on Jack Frost's head. The fairies watched as it rolled down his pouty face. Suddenly, his fierce face changed. He seemed to shiver. "Of course I'll give you back the leaf," he said, placing it in Autumn's hand. At once, the leaf shrunk to Autumn's size. "I just thought more winter would be more fun. I don't know how it got out of control." Rachel and Kirsty exchanged glances. Jack Frost seemed truly sorry.

He looked down. The water was now up to his knobby knees. The castle was still melting. The spiky turrets were gone, and the magnificent Ice Castle now looked more like a sloppy ice fort. Jack Frost returned his gaze to Autumn. "Aren't you going to go?" he asked, his voice soft and uncertain. "You have your leaf. Shouldn't you check on the human world?"

"I think my good friends can take care of that," Autumn said, nodding at Rachel and Kirsty. She turned back to Jack Frost. "You and I have work to do. It will take all of our magic to reverse this melting spell."

Jack Frost's eyes grew big. "Thank you," he whispered. "I would be grateful."

Rachel and Kirsty looked at each other. After everything that had happened, Jack Frost and Autumn were going to work together. It would take a lot of teamwork to make things right again.

A Perfect Fall Day

Autumn quicky thanked Rachel and
Kirsty, and gave her wand a fancy twirl.
"Make sure fall has finally come to the
human world," she said as a glittering
cloud fell over the girls. A sparkly
whirlwind carried the girls out of the
castle and over Fairyland. The castle
wasn't much more than a mound of ice,

and there was water everywhere. "Even Fairyland Forest is flooded," Rachel said with concern. Then the girls felt a familiar tingle in their finger and toes.

Almost instantly, Rachel and Kirsty were back in their world—and back to being girls. The next thing they noticed was what was under their feet: leaves! There were lots and lots of colorful leaves everywhere! The girls could see adults and kids raking them into a pile.

Everything seemed to be coming together here, but the girls knew that Autumn and Jack Frost were still working to fix things in Fairyland.

"It's almost time for the leaf jump," Kirsty said, looking at her watch.

"Let's help them get ready," said Rachel.

The friends helped rake more leaves into the gully. With everyone raking, it filled up quickly. When Kyra, the farmer, announced it was time to start jumping, Kirsty and Rachel got in line. They were filled with nervous energy. "I'm excited to jump," Kirsty admitted, "but I'm also worried about Autumn and Fairyland."

Rachel nodded. She knew just how her friend felt. She was glad that the Fall Festival was such a success, and that there were plenty of leaves for the Great Leaf Leap, but she was thinking about Fairyland as well. When it was their turn, Rachel and Kirsty climbed the steps to the platform. They held hands, looked at each other, and counted. "One, two, three!" they chanted, and they leaped down together. Their feet plunged into the pile with a *crash* and a *crunch*. The girls laughed, surrounded with the bright colors of fall.

"Let's do it again!" Rachel cried as they stumbled out of the gully.

"Yes, let's!" As Kirsty pulled a leaf from her hair, something caught her eye. "Hey, look over there, in the woods."

Rachel searched the colorful trees until her eyes rested on a bright, glittering light. "I'll bet it's Autumn," she whispered.

The girls ran toward the magical glow, hoping to see their friend.

"Autumn!" Kirsty called once they reached the edge of the forest.

"Hello, girls!" Autumn cried. "I'm very tired from helping Jack Frost rebuild the Ice Castle, but I wanted to come thank you for all your help."

"We were happy to," Rachel said.

Autumn handed each girl a tiny gift wrapped in red foil.

As the girls pulled on the gold ribbons, the presents sprang to human-size. Inside, Rachel and Kirsty each found a beautiful handwoven scarf. Kirsty's was

striped red and orange, Rachel's yellow
and red.

"They're beautiful!" the girls
exclaimed, and they both put them on.

"May they keep you warm and safe,
whatever the seasons bring," Autumn
said with a smile. "I have to go now, but
I hope you enjoy the rest of the festival."

She rose into the air and waved her wand.

"Thank you!" Kirsty and Rachel called as they waved good-bye. Autumn was now a twirling, glittery cloud.

The girls turned to walk back to the Fall Festival. New Growth Farm was a vision of fall beauty, with colorful trees, the wind rustling the leaves, and baskets of fruit and vegetables everywhere. "It doesn't feel like it could be true," Kirsty said.

"I know," Rachel agreed. "Now everything seems perfect."

"This is just how fall should be,"

agreed Kirsty. "And, thanks to Autumn, we should have a fabulous, snowy winter, and a fresh, cheery spring, followed by a warm, sunny summer."

"Let's just hope Jack Frost learned his lesson and will leave the seasons alone," Rachel said.

"I hope so," Kirsty agreed, snuggling in her lovely striped scarf. "Because nature really is magical."

SPECIAL EDITION

Don't miss any of Rachel and Kirsty's
other fairy adventures!
Check out this magical sneak peek of

Keira
the Movie Star Fairy!

Read on for a special sneak peek. . . .

Setting the Scene

"Look, there's Julianna Stewart!" whispered Kirsty Tate. "Isn't her fairy princess costume beautiful?"

Rachel Walker peeked around just as Julianna walked past. The movie star gave the girls a friendly wink, then sat down in a director's chair with her name on the back to study her script.

"I can't believe a really famous actress like Julianna would come to Wetherbury village," said Rachel.

"And I can't believe that she's spending most of our school vacation in Mrs. Croft's garden!" added Kirsty.

Mrs. Croft was a friend of Kirsty's parents, a sweet old lady who had lived in Wetherbury for years. Her little thatched cottage with pretty, blossoming trees in the front yard often caught the eyes of tourists and passersby. A few weeks ago when Mrs. Croft had been working in her garden, an executive from a big movie studio had pulled up outside. He wanted to use the cottage in a brand-new movie starring the famous actress Julianna Stewart. When Mrs. Croft agreed, she became the talk of the village! Trucks full of set designers, lighting engineers, and prop-makers had turned up to transform her garden into a magical world. Now, filming on *The Starlight Chronicles* was about to begin.

"It was so nice of Mrs. Croft to let us spend some time on the set," said Rachel, watching the director talk through the next scene with his star.

Not only had Mrs. Croft arranged for the friends to watch the rehearsals, but when she'd heard that Rachel was coming to stay with Kirsty for a week, the kind old lady had also managed to get the girls parts as extras!

The pair had been cast as magical fairies, helpers to Julianna's fairy princess in one of the most exciting scenes in the movie. It was the perfect part for them both—Kirsty and Rachel knew a lot about fairies! The two best friends had been secretly visiting Fairyland for a while. They never knew when one of the fairies would need their help, but they were always ready to protect their magical friends from Jack Frost and his troublesome goblins.

"I can't wait to try on our costumes," said Kirsty. "I wonder if they'll be as beautiful as real fairy clothes."

Rachel shook her head and smiled. All the sequins and glitter in the human world couldn't look as magical as a real fairy fluttering in her finery! Before she could answer her friend, the director tapped his clipboard with a pen.

"Attention, everybody," he called. "I'd like to run this scene from the top. We start filming first thing tomorrow and there's still lots of work to do."

Kirsty and Rachel exchanged excited looks as the set bustled with people. Helpers known as "runners" got props for the actors and showed the extras where to stand. Sound and lighting experts rigged up cables, while the dancers practiced their steps. In this scene of *The Starlight Chronicles*, the fairy princess was due to greet the prince at a sparkling moonlit ball.

Kirsty and Rachel couldn't wait to hear the stars run through their lines! They watched as Julianna took her place in front of Chad Stenning, the actor cast as the fairy prince.

"And . . . action!" cried the director, giving a thumbs-up.

Julianna coughed shyly, then stepped forward.

"Your Highness," she said, making a dainty curtsy. "The air shimmers with enchantment this evening. Shall we dance?"

Chad bowed. "Let the music wait a while. Please walk with me on the terrace. There is something I must say."

The crew watched, spellbound, as Chad offered his arm to Julianna and led her off the set.

"Excellent work!" announced the director, making a note on his clipboard. "Let's take five."

Rachel and Kirsty chatted while the cast took a quick break. Runners rushed around the director, collecting notes and passing messages to the crew.

"I haven't seen that runner before," whispered Rachel, nudging her friend's arm. "He seems to be in a big hurry."

Kirsty looked up as the runner elbowed his way past the actors, then snatched a script from the director's table. She tried to see his face, but it was hidden under a dark baseball cap. It was only when he bumped her chair on the way out of the garden that she spotted a glimpse of green skin.

"That's no runner," Kirsty said breathlessly. "It's a goblin!"

★   ★   ★

Rachel felt the back of her neck begin to tingle. If Jack Frost's goblins were in Wetherbury, it could mean nothing but trouble! She followed Kirsty's gaze and saw that, sure enough, two warty green feet were poking out of the bottom of the stranger's jeans.

"That's a goblin all right," she said. "We'd better follow him!"

Kirsty nodded and jumped to her feet, just as the director called "Action!" one more time. Before the girls could slip away, a group of actors rushed forward to act out a party scene in the enchanted garden.

"Good evening, Your Highness," piped up a girl in a fairy skirt.

The man next to her elbowed the girl in the ribs and hissed, "That's *my* line, silly!"

The director rolled his eyes. "Take it from the top, please."

"Attention, fairies! Sinner is derved," babbled the man. "Oh, no! I mean 'dinner is served'! Or does that line come later? I can't remember!"

"Let's move on." The director frowned, turning to Chad and Julianna.

The cast and crew waited for the leading man and lady to start speaking. But instead of saying their lines, they stayed totally silent.

"Julianna?" called the director. "Julianna!"

Julianna looked helplessly at Chad.

"Is it m–me next?" she stuttered. "My mind's gone blank!"

The set fell into chaos as assistants scrambled to track down the correct page in the script.

"I don't understand," whispered Rachel. "Chad and Julianna have been perfect up until now. Something has gone terribly wrong."

"We have to find that goblin! I bet he has something to do with all this," Kirsty said.

Rachel pointed to a path made of stepping-stones that curved around the back of Mrs. Croft's cottage. "He ran down there. Let's go!"